Congratulations on choosing the best in educational materials for your child. By selecting top-quality McGraw-Hill products, you can be assured that the concepts used in our books will reinforce and enhance the skills that are being taught in classrooms nationwide.

And what better way to get young readers excited than with Mercer Mayer's Little Critter, a character loved by children everywhere? Our First Readers offer simple and engaging stories about Little Critter that children can read on their own. Each level incorporates reading skills, colorful illustrations, and challenging activities.

Level 1 – The stories are simple and use repetitive language. Illustrations are highly supportive.
Level 2 - The stories begin to grow in complexity. Language is still repetitive, but it is mixed with more challenging vocabulary.
Level 3 - The stories are more complex. Sentences are longer and more varied.

To help your child make the most of this book, look at the first few pictures in the story and discuss what is happening. Ask your child to predict where the story is going. Then, once your child has read the story, have him or her review the word list and do the activities. This will reinforce vocabulary words from the story and build reading comprehension.

You are your child's first and most influential teacher. No one knows your child the way you do. Tailor your time together to reinforce a newly acquired skill or to overcome a temporary stumbling block. Praise your child's progress and ideas, take delight in his or her imagination, and most of all, enjoy your time together!

Mc Graw Hill McGraw-Hill Children's Publishing

Send all inquiries to:
McGraw-Hill Children's Publishing
8787 Orion Place
Columbus, OH 43240-4027

Printed in the United States of America.

1-57768-845-7

 A Big Tuna Trading Company, LLC/J. R. Sansevere Book

Library of Congress Cataloging-in-Publication Data is on file with the publisher.

1 2 3 4 5 6 7 8 9 10 PHXBK 07 06 05 04 03 02

The McGraw-Hill Companies

Level **3**   Grades **1–2**

CLASS TRIP

by Mercer Mayer

**McGraw-Hill
Children's Publishing**

Columbus, Ohio

Today we went on a class trip.
We went to the science museum.

It was a lot of fun,
and we learned a whole lot.

5

First, we saw the dinosaurs.
"This is a model of a Tyrannosaurus
  Rex," Miss Kitty told us.
"He lived about 90 million years ago."
  I pressed a button. The dinosaur roared.
  It was really loud, but I wasn't scared.

Then, we went to see a model
of the planet Mars.
Mars has craters like the moon.

"Look at that weird car," said Tiger.
"It is like the real one they used
on Mars," said Miss Kitty.
We took turns using the remote control
to make it go.

After that, we went into a dark room.
We sat down. Miss Kitty told us
to look up.
"Wow! Look at all the stars," I said.
"The Big Dipper is over there," said Gabby.
"It looks like a big spoon."

Then, we went into a room
called Rainbows.

Miss Kitty handed each of us a crystal.
"White light is made up of all the colors
  of the rainbow," she said.
"Crystals break up the light."
We held up our crystals. Mine covered
Tiger with rainbow stripes.

Next, we went to a room that had glass walls. It had lots of plants, too. Suddenly, a butterfly landed on me. "Look!" I cried.

"That butterfly is tasting you," said Miss Kitty. "Butterflies taste with their feet."

Finally, it was time to go home.
"I want to come back and see the stars,"
said Gabby.
"I want to come back and see the
dinosaurs," said Tiger.
"I want to come back and see
everything," I said.
Science is a lot of fun!

Word List

Read each word in the lists below. Then, find each word in the story. Now, make up a new sentence using the word. Say your sentence out loud.

Words I Know

dinosaurs
button
planet
stars
rainbow
plants

Challenge Words

science
museum
scared
weird
crystals
suddenly

What Did You Learn?

Point to the sentences below that tell things you learned from the story. Try not to look back at the story.

Tyrannosaurus Rex lived 90 million years ago.

There are crystals in the craters on the moon.

Mars has craters like the moon.

Stars are made up of crystals.

Butterflies taste things with their feet.

Crystals break up light into rainbows.

Verbs

To change some verbs so they describe something that happened in the past, you must add ed to the end of the word.

Now: I want ice cream.
In the past: Yesterday, I wanted ice cream.

To change other verbs so they describe something that happened in the past, you must change the whole word.

Now: I sit on a barber shop chair.
In the past: Last week, I sat on a barber
               shop chair.

The verbs in the left-hand column are happening now. The verbs in the right-hand column are happening in the past. Using your finger, match the verbs on the left to their partners on the right.

sit	ran
do	was
take	went
tell	did
run	took
go	told
is	sat

Homophones: There/Their

Some words sound the same even though they mean different things and have different spellings. These words are called homophones.

There and their are homophones.

Example:

I live over there.

Maurice and Molly are playing on their swings.

How many times did you see the word there in the story?

How many times did you see the word their in the story?

Read the sentences below. Point to the sentence that uses the correct form of there or their.

Hit the ball over there.

Hit the ball over their.

Maurice and Molly packed there lunches.

Maurice and Molly packed their lunches.

Let's play over there!

Let's play over their!

Little Critter and Little Sister wore there pajamas to bed.

Little Critter and Little Sister wore their pajamas to bed.

Answer Key

page 19
What Did I Learn?

Tyrannosaurus Rex lived 90 million years ago.

There are crystals in the craters on the moon.

Mars has craters like the moon.

Stars are made up of crystals.

Butterflies taste things with their feet.

Crystals break up light into rainbows.

page 21
Verbs

sit   ran

do   was

take   went

tell   did

run   took

go   told

is   sat

page 22
Homophones: There/Their

How many times did you see the word there in the story? 1

How many times did you see the word their in the story? 1

page 23
Homophones: There/Their

Hit the ball over there.
Hit the ball over their.

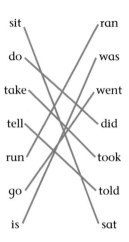

Maurice and Molly packed there lunches.
Maurice and Molly packed their lunches.

Let's play over there!
Let's play over their!

Little Critter and Little Sister wore there pajamas to bed.
Little Critter and Little Sister wore their pajamas to bed.